Moose On A Mission

By
Michael MacCurtain

Illustrated By Stan Jaskeil

Printed in Korea by asianprinting.com

ISBN: 978-0-615-44313-3

About the Author:

Michael MacCurtain is a retired schoolteacher who wrote his first
Willie The Moose story for his students in Natick, Massachusetts.
He enjoys reading his stories to his own grandchildren.
He makes his home in Whitman, Massachusetts.
He can be reached at mpmaccurtain@yahoo.com

About the Illustrator:

Stan Jaskeil is a highly regarded illustrator from Salem, Massachusetts.
His work can be seen at his website stanjaskielcartoons.com.
He can be reached at SJTOONS@aol.com

For Wanda – Whose encouragement and support have made these books possible

"Hey ranger, hey ranger," Ranger Roy heard the sound
And the forest ranger knew his friend Willie was around.

Now a talking moose may seem very strange,
But that was a gift Saint Nick had arranged.
And so, in the North Woods, on this warm spring day,
The ranger was there to hear Willie say,
"Ranger Roy, Ranger Roy I had a terrible dream
Of a day when our North woods were no longer green,

When our rivers were brown all the blue was gone
And we no longer heard our feathered friends song!
The Beavers couldn't build, the Robins couldn't nest
And life in our forest was no longer the best!

No leaves on the trees, all the branches were bare,
And worst of all, no one seemed to care!

So when I awoke I came here on the double
To tell you I know that our North Woods are in trouble.

We must all help out, we must all lend a hand,
Right here in the North Woods we must take a stand.
All the creatures of the forest must help or I fear
The North Woods we all love will soon disappear!

A meeting was called, all the animals were there,
From the tiniest Chipmunk to the great Grizzly Bear
Willie spoke calmly though he wanted to scream
As he told all his friends of his terrible dream.
"Our woodland needs help to stay as it's been,
We must all pitch in to keep our home green.
For the plants and the trees to continue to thrive
All the creatures must help keep the forest alive"

The Squirrels and Chipmunks then offered with a titter
To round up, collect and gather all litter

The Deer spoke up next and said that each night
They would make it a point to check all campsites
To make sure fires were out and each campsite was clean.
That was their way of helping to keep our woods green.

The Hawks said they'd watch the rivers and streams
To see that the Humans kept our waterways clean.
The Moose and the Bear said they'd guard against danger,
And when they saw trouble they'd go tell the ranger.

Ranger Roy then promised, "I'll work very hard,
I'll treat the North Woods like it was my backyard.
For if man caused these problems then it's only right,
That man should help you in your ecological fight."

Then the smallest of birds had the idea of the hour
"We'll use the petals of the Great North Woods flowers
To make a sign by all Humans seen"

DATE DUE

MAR 11 '8 8		NOV 7 '95	23
		NOV 15 '95	23
12	MAY 26 '95	APR 29 '98	4
12	APR 1 '91	SEP 24	
		MAY 06 '97	
17	OCT 27 '92	NOV 20	
12	NOV 13 '92	FEB 11 '90	
9	NOV 18 '92	SE 25	
17	FEB 9 '93	JA 10 '01	
22	JAN 18 '93	OR 4 '02	
18	APR 25 '94	SEP 19 '08	
14	OCT 17 '94	SEP 19 '06	
8	MAR 23 '95	MAY 18 '07	
10	APR 27 '95	MAR 20 '09	
9	MAY 26 '95	MAR 1	
10			
24	OCT 19 '95		

DEMCO 38-297

Klaus Paysan

DOMESTIC PETS

Lerner Publications Company
Minneapolis, Minnesota

The Library of Congress cataloged the original printing of this title as follows:

Paysan, Klaus.
    Domestic pets. [English translation by Susan Hegele-Bollinger] Minneapolis, Lerner Publications Co. [1972, c1971]
    112 p. illus. (part col.) 22 x 25 cm.
    SUMMARY: Text and photographs introduce various species of dogs, cats, birds, fish, and other animals and the care they need as pets.
    Translation of Unsere liebsten Tiere.
    1. Pets — Juvenile literature. [1. Pets] I. Title.

SF416.2.P3813 1972   636.08′87   73-171531
ISBN 0-8225-0566-5   MARC
                                                      AC

A NATURE AND MAN BOOK

Second Printing 1978

First published in the United States 1972 by Lerner Publications Company, Minneapolis, Minnesota. All English language rights reserved.
Published simultaneously in Canada by J. M. Dent & Sons Ltd., Don Mills, Ontario.
Copyright © MCMLXXI by Deutsche Verlags-Anstalt, Stuttgart, Germany.

International Standard Book Number: 0-8225-0566-5
Library of Congress Catalog Card Number: 73-171531

Manufactured in the United States of America.

CONTENTS

Introduction 5
House Cat 8
Siamese Cat 10
Training a Cat 12
Persian Cat 12
Wire-haired Dachshund 14
Selecting and
    Raising a Dog 16
French Bulldog 16
Fox Terrier 18
Boxer 20
Cocker Spaniel 22
Poodle 24
Saluki 26
Collie 28
German Shepherd 30
Schnauzer 32
Saint Bernard 34
Great Dane 36

Pekingese 38
Pomeranian 40
Rhesus Monkey 42
Monkey 44
Squirrel Monkey 46
Bush Baby 48
Guinea Pig 50
White Mouse 52
Golden Hamster 54
Squirrel 56
Chipmunk 58
Horse 60
Pony 62
Donkey 64
Parakeet 66
Lovebirds 68
Amazon Parrot and
    Blunt-tailed Parrot 70
Scarlet Macaw 72

Chinese Nightingale 74
Mynah 76
Magpie 78
Canary 80
European Goldfinch 82
Siskin 84
Butterfly Finch 86
Mandarin Duck 88
Emerald Lizard 90
Tree Frog 92
Turtle 94
Tortoise 96
Goldfish 98
Guppy 100
Paradise Fish 102
Angelfish 104
All about the Animals 106

INTRODUCTION

Our friends in the animal kingdom create an atmosphere of warmth and love that is especially welcome in the modern world. How many people who have felt useless or left out of society have gained new strength and hope from a faithful dog? But dogs are not the only animals which can help remove our loneliness with their loyalty and affection. Nature has created many kinds of animals which can live comfortably with us and bring real pleasure to our lives.

Some animals need a lot of room, some are noisy, some have a strong smell. Some animals are expensive to buy and have delicate health; others cost very little and are always robust. Future pet owners need to know and consider the characteristics of all the animals before deciding which pet will share their home for many years. Since the development of air freight, pet shops and dealers have been able to offer a great variety of species for sale. Today almost no pet is unobtainable; even elephants can be bought at department stores.

That reminds me of the experience of a friend of mine, a German prince in Portuguese West Africa. One day some hunters made him a present of a few-days-old baby elephant. As my friend had a cattle ranch, finding food for the elephant was no problem, and he accepted the present. The first night, the young elephant was shut in with the cows, but it became homesick and began to cry piercingly. The prince felt that he had no choice but to have a pile of straw put beside his bed and to hold the little elephant's trunk comfortingly. As soon as the prince fell asleep the elephant climbed up on the bed beside his protector. And that is how things stayed, night after night. "I strengthened the legs of the bed twice, and in the end I put my mattress on the floor," said the prince. "I also had to have the stairs strengthened. Three years later, just as I was wondering how I could strengthen the floors so that the now very heavy elephant would not fall through them, the elephant suddenly died. I was very unhappy, and it was a long time before I got used to an empty bed again."

The prince's story shows that the most important question when choosing an animal is not how much one likes it or how cute it is, but how easy or difficult it will be to live with as the years go by. The little, ordinary things are the important ones: Does the animal make much noise, does it smell, does it bite, does it create a lot of dirt, will the rest of the family like living with it? Many problems may arise if we take a liking to a chimpanzee or a gorilla, for example, or even if we allow a large dog to sleep in our bedroom. A macaw is a beautiful bird, but it can ruin the nerves of everyone around it with its shrill calls. A skunk whose stink gland is still intact will obviously not be popular with anyone.

There are many other things to be considered before selecting a pet. If we choose the animal wisely, we will have many years of happiness. But our decision should not be made too quickly. One important question is housing. Do we have enough space for this animal? What equipment will it need to feel comfortable and happy? Some pets need large cages or large yards to play in, whereas other animals are perfectly happy staying inside the house.

The personalities of the animals must also be carefully considered. A quiet and domestic person should never buy a dog which would want to run for two hours a day. People who are sensitive to noise should beware of buying a dog like the schnauzer, for whom barking is an essential part of life. Those who like organizing and giving orders will find little pleasure in a cat. A cat will always be loyal to the family, but independence is part of its nature. The person who keeps a cat must be willing to let it come to him for affection when it wants to. A cat needs freedom to be tame, but a dog needs sternness as well as love. In selecting a pet, remember that animals which in nature live alone will react as cats do when they are in captivity, whereas herd animals will react as dogs do. A quiet person may find pleasure in fish. He will soon see that, in spite of the glass wall around them and their completely different environment, fish are not as cold and distant as they are sometimes said to be. Many a fish breeder has succeeded in building a personal relationship with his cichlid or anabantid. Birds and lizards are good pets for people who prefer more contact with their pets.

We also must consider what will happen to our animals at vacation time. Can we always take the pet with us—even across national boundaries? Or will we have difficulty finding a friend or a suitable kennel we can leave it with? Will the animal make us so tied to our home that we will be unable to go anywhere?

It is also important to remember that our beloved pet, especially if it is a small one, will die after a few years. Few domestic animals reach such an age that they survive us. Some people decide never to have a pet just for this reason. But death is natural. And if you ask yourself what is more important, the years of pleasure you will have with the animal or the brief pain at its death, you will probably decide that the pleasure and the happy memories are worth more.

Where can you buy your future companion? Pedigreed dogs and cats can be bought from a breeder. Addresses of breeders can be obtained from dog or cat clubs or from catalogs of animal shows. It is best to visit the breeder personally. He will explain how to train the dog or cat and tell you the special characteristics of the animal you have chosen. Horses and donkeys can be purchased from breeders or dealers whose addresses are given out by riding clubs. These clubs are also a good source of information about veterinarians and stabling facilities. Rodents, birds, reptiles, fish, and small exotic animals can be bought in pet shops. You should, however, buy animals only in a shop that is extremely clean. Wherever you buy an animal, be sure to consult a veterinarian about proper health care and special diet needs.

Every kind of animal has to be treated differently. Some animals must be left in their cages, and you must simply observe their behavior. Others can be let out, and you can try to learn about their character by playing with them. No matter which kind of pet you choose, remember that all of them have sensitive feelings, just as human beings have. They quickly pine away if they are given only food and water and otherwise neglected. The higher the stage of development in the animal, the more attention you must give it if you want to receive its affection. However, any animal in your home deserves all of the love and care you can give it.

KLAUS PAYSAN

House Cat

Almost everyone has an opinion about dogs and cats. Some people like dogs, others like cats, and seldom do people feel strong affection for both of these completely opposite characters. The dog is a herd animal which easily adjusts to family life and will be faithful to its master until death. The cat, on the other hand, remains an individualist and is usually more attached to the house than its owner. A cat will come purring for affection when it wants to, but it will go off on its own when tired of being in the house. Seldom will a cat obey commands. However, these characteristics—an independent spirit and a slightly wild nature—are the ones that delight cat lovers all over the world. Who can resist a cat when it begins purring and rubbing affectionately against one's legs (even when it has just slyly stolen a piece of meat)? "They fight like cats and dogs" is often said of people who cannot stand the sight of each other. Actually, cats and dogs can be the best of friends if they get used to each other while they are young. A dog becomes aggressive only when it senses its master's dislike of cats, and then a cat naturally acts to protect itself. Since old cats do not change their habits very easily, it is best to buy a young kitten, one that is about two months old. The kitten should be vaccinated right away against distemper, a disease that is usually fatal. Keeping a cat in the city is not as easy as one might think. First of all, a cat must be housebroken. To do this, fill a box or a pan with dry dirt or sand. As soon as the cat begins to look around searchingly, especially after a meal, place it in the box. The cat will soon learn to go to the box by itself. The sand must be changed regularly; a cat will not return to a place that is too dirty. It is also necessary to feed a cat carefully. A saucer of milk is not enough to give it proper nourishment. A cat must have meat, either fresh or canned, to replace the mice it would catch in the country. Cats like to play, and space must be provided for this. Kittens practice catching things, and their mother brings them live mice to play with. If you have only one kitten, give it a suitable replacement for a mouse, such as a ball of yarn or a rubber mouse. Also, cats have a tendency to sharpen their claws on the furniture. They should have their own scratching bar, perhaps a piece of carpet nailed to a wooden post.

Siamese Cat

The Siamese cat is one of the pedigreed breeds of cat. Although these cats were kept in the palaces and temples of Thailand (Siam) for centuries, they are by no means lazy or overly tame. On the contrary, they are often wilder than other domestic cats. Both male and female Siamese cats have an unusual, mournful cry. Many a cat owner has had to send his pets into the country during the mating season because their low, haunting "meows" have got on the neighbors' nerves. After an eight-week period of gestation the female Siamese gives birth to between four and six kittens. They have hardly any fur at first, and their eyes do not open fully until the ninth day. In contrast to the adult cats, which have dark faces and feet, Siamese kittens are completely white. Their coloring changes as they grow, and within a year they are the same colors as their parents. All Siamese cats have lovely clear blue eyes. Those with dark brown "points" (ears, face, paws, and tail) are known as seal-points. A less common type of Siamese is the blue-point, which has a blue white body and bluish brown points. The Siamese and all other cats can probably trace their ancestry to a cat like the fallow, or yellow, cat (drawn at left), which still lives wild in parts of Asia and Africa.

12 Persian Cat

Training a Cat

By nature, a domestic cat is an animal of prey, just like its close relatives the lion, tiger, and leopard. Just the opposite of a dog, who stalks his prey like a typical hunter, a cat lies in wait when it is hunting. Or the most it will do is creep up on its prey and grab the animal with a quick jump. A cat kills its prey by biting it sharply at the neck. If a cat has young, she brings the kittens injured prey so that they can practice their hunting methods. She shows them how to sneak up on the animal and spring at it. They do not kill it but let it run away and then pounce on it over and over again. This game is necessary even though it is cruel, for only in this way can the kittens learn to hunt correctly. Older kittens who have practiced hunting catch their prey and kill it quite rapidly. If full-grown cats continue to torture their prey, they should be punished until the habit is broken. A cat who is allowed to run freely around the neighborhood may also need careful training. If it proudly brings home a bird, the dead animal should be taken away with a show of disgust. If it brings home a second bird, the cat should be hit lightly on the ears. That certainly should stop it from repeating the offense.

The beautiful Persian cat is also called an Angora or a longhair. It is a little more delicate than other breeds of cat and cannot be allowed to run free very often, as seeds and burrs easily become caught in its long coat. The Persian also needs more grooming than other cats; the coat is so long that the cat's tongue and paws alone cannot make it shine. The lovely soft fur should be combed and brushed every day to keep it from becoming matted. Persian cats come in all colors, mostly in the paler shades. One variety is pure white with one blue and one green eye. Persians need a great deal of affection and purr happily when they receive it. They enjoy being stroked as they lie comfortably on a soft chair or, better still, on their owner's lap. Although they can creep around silently on their soft paws, these cats, like other breeds, have needle-sharp claws which they extend when danger approaches. All cats like to play, and since the Persian cannot be out of doors very much and does not have much change of scene, it must have enough room inside in which to play.

Wire-haired Dachshund

Many jokes have been made about the obedience of dachshunds. It has been said that the command they will obey best is "Are you coming or not?" But their stubbornness is not really as bad as some people think. A dachshund must simply be trained with the same care that a hunter uses to train his hunting dog. The dachshund is considered to be the national dog of Germany. It was bred originally as a hunting dog, and the name is German for badger hound. Since the dachshund is so small, it can creep into a fox's or a badger's hole and attack the animal where it is hiding. Besides the wire-haired dachshund, there are several other varieties of this breed, including the long-haired and the smooth-haired. The smooth-haired dachshund, with a tan coat, is quite common in the United States. All dachshunds are alert and hardy, and they have a good sense of smell. But they have one very bad habit, that of chewing shoes and rugs. This can be avoided by giving them their own things to chew. Rolled "bones" made from rawhide or buffalo skin make good chewing toys; they remain hard for a long time but finally soften and can be eaten.

16 French Bulldog

Selecting and Raising a Dog

It is best to buy a dog when it is 10 to 15 weeks old. At this age the puppy is still so helpless that it really needs a family in which it can feel protected. A young dog adapts itself well to the family social unit, and its behavior is easily shaped by its owner. When buying a dog, it is better to look at the quality of the animal than at the price. Mongrels eat just as much as pedigreed dogs, and the cost of feeding and caring for a dog is much higher than the initial purchase price. It is fun to buy a "mutt" and see what kind of dog the tiny, helpless ball of wool develops into. On the other hand, it is just as fun to choose from the hundreds of purebred dogs one which seems to be ideal in terms of behavior and size. Another reason to choose a pedigreed dog is that they have been carefully bred for a life in human society. The breeder has fed them well and has had them wormed and vaccinated against distemper. Also, a look at the dog's parents will show exactly what it will be like some day soon. People who do not have much money should not consider buying a large dog

(Continued on page 18)

French bulldogs are alert and lively and make good watchdogs—all visitors to their house are greeted with loud barking. They are typical indoor dogs, not needing much exercise and not caring for long walks (their bodies are not made for hard work). Great care must be taken of their figures. French bulldogs should not be slim; their bodies should be sturdy and solid, weighing 18 to 28 pounds. However, if they develop too many rolls of fat, these faithful dogs will soon be plagued with all the disorders that come with excess weight and inactivity in animals—disease of the heart, liver, and kidneys, as well as asthmatic complaints. The tendency to gain weight can be counteracted by encouraging French bulldogs to play. They especially like playing with balls, and if they started playing with them when young, their games are likely to be exciting. The French bulldog becomes very attached to the members of the family and is considered quite intelligent. This breed is about half the size of the English bulldog and has a more pleasant face.

Fox Terrier

like the Great Dane or Saint Bernard; they eat too much food. People who have a small home also should not buy a large dog. There is a suitable breed of dog for everyone, for people who like taking walks and for people who are lazy, for people who like giving orders and expect complete obedience and for people who are more tolerant and want individuality in a dog.

When the young puppy is first brought home, its feeding and water bowls should be ready and waiting. Its bed, a foam rubber pad covered with a washable rough fabric, should also be in its place. The first day in a strange place is a difficult time for the puppy. It should be stroked gently in its bed and given a few tasty tidbits. The dog will sniff at the shoes of its new owners and may be given worn, unwashed socks in bed. This way the puppy can get used to the smell of its new owners and locate them even if it cannot see them. (Dogs, with the exception of certain kinds of hounds, depend more on their sense of smell than on their eyesight.) Once the puppy has been brought

(Continued on page 20)

In contrast to French bulldogs, fox terriers have long, straight legs well suited for running. These dogs are too lively for some people. They are always dashing around the house, wanting to play a game, and they also enjoy barking. However, they do not bark as loud or as often as schnauzers do. There are two kinds of fox terrier, the wire-haired, which is shown in the photograph, and the smooth-coated, which today is quite rare. Bred by the English for hunting foxes, fox terriers are true daredevils and, if the need arises, good rat and mouse hunters. Since they are so lively and fearless, they are sometimes used in zoos to nurse young tigers and lions. The young cubs are even allowed to drink the terrier's milk. Until they are completely grown, several large, heavy cats can be kept under control by one female fox terrier. Fox terriers reach a maximum weight of 18 pounds and live to about the age of 14. They should be fed meat and an occasional egg, as well as oats and vegetables. Wire-haired fox terriers must be clipped regularly. A cloth-covered foam cushion is quite adequate for their bed.

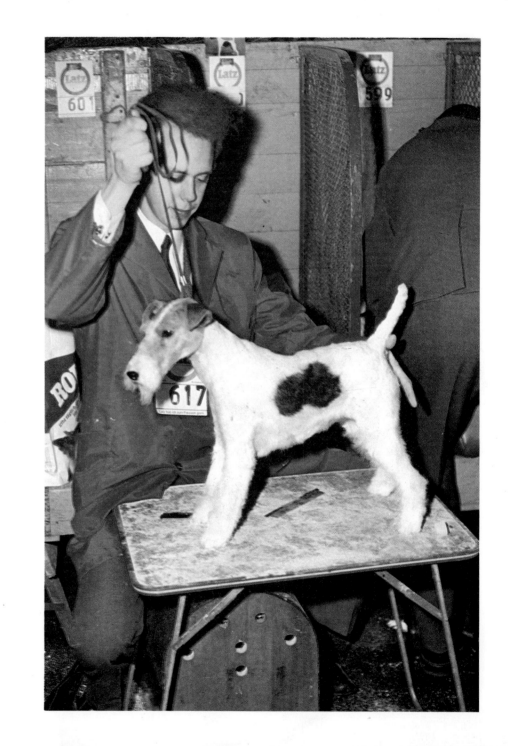

Boxer

The boxer is a good protector and watchdog which defends its owner's home and property against unwelcome visitors. It attacks fearlessly and can bite viciously with its powerful lower jaw. Although boxers look frightening and move quickly, they are really very patient, especially with children in their owner's family. They must, however, be trained to complete obedience because of their size and strength. Full-grown boxers weigh 60 to 75 pounds. Long walks and strenuous exercise are necessary to keep them in good form. A well-trained, muscular boxer is still a good-looking animal at the age of seven, but an overweight three-year-old is, on the other hand, a catastrophe. Boxers are easy to care for because of their short coat, and they hardly ever smell, although they may start to drool when they are older. The short nose has been especially bred, and it is a surprising contrast to the pointed nose of the jackal, one of the boxer's relatives. The jackal (drawn at left), the wolf, and the bulldog are considered the probable ancestors of the boxer.

home, a period of careful training must follow. It takes a great deal of time and patience to train a dog so that later its behavior will exactly match what is expected. The most important thing is to get the dog housebroken. As soon as the little puppy becomes restless, it should be picked up and carried out of doors. It should be kept there until it has performed. Afterwards, the dog should be praised warmly and then returned inside. If the puppy has an accident in the house, it should immediately be taken to the scene of the crime. Then its nose should be placed close to the spot, and the puppy should be scolded. The puppy's nose should never be rubbed in the spot, as this would be a humiliation for the dog and could fill it with hate for its new master. Soon the

(Continued on page 22)

Cocker Spaniel

dog will know the proper place out of doors and will even learn to tell its owners when it needs to go out.

The next point concerns general hygiene. Never, not even on the first day at home, should a dog be allowed to lie on the bed. The couch and chairs should also be out of bounds. The same applies to a dining table. Even if it is very amusing the first time the dog steals the Sunday roast, such a bad habit will bring certain unhappiness in the future. It is best never to give the dog anything while the family is eating; then the animal will not form the annoying habit of begging. Nothing is more unpleasant for a visitor than a dog which thinks it has the right to beg. In general, a dog should not have any contact at all with its owners' food. Licking of the hands or the face should also be strictly forbidden from the start. It is especially important that the dog be taught how to act with small children. Licking the child or accepting food from him should not be allowed.

(Continued on page 24)

Cocker spaniels are hunting dogs by nature, bred in England to hunt birds called woodcocks. Today most cockers are not used for hunting but kept as pets. The spaniel's size and disposition place it in the group of dogs which can be called house dogs: It grows to about 16 inches in height at the shoulder and has a gentle, affectionate manner. Cockers are even suitable as city dogs. However, they need a lot of exercise, because of their origins, and they should have at least two walks a day. If cockers are kept in town, great care should be taken that their food does not make them too fat. A cocker has a long coat that should be brushed well each day. In spring the dog will shed its extra winter coat, and you may have trouble keeping the house tidy. But any trouble is quickly forgotten when you receive one loving glance from the cocker's large dark eyes. In recent years breeders have obtained several fashionable color variations of this appealing dog. The red color is especially popular.

Poodle

Young puppies may snap at the arms and legs of their human friends in play. To keep this playful biting from having more unpleasant consequences when the dog is older and does not know its own strength, discourage all biting right away. Rebuke the dog sharply, and if necessary push the dog's lips between its teeth. These actions will give the animal such a dislike for biting that this bad habit will never develop. Of course, this kind of training is wrong for watchdogs and guard dogs, but then they are never family pets. Formal training for a dog should begin when it is about a year old. Watchdogs and guard dogs should be given to a professional trainer, but a less thorough training is enough for housepets. In any large town there are obedience schools, where trainers teach housepets and their owners how to live together without conflict. Only cruel people beat their animals. Gentle owners work with praise and rebuke, with rewards and punishment. However, they make sure that every command is obeyed; otherwise the dog will get out of hand and become the master of the house.

Poodles originated in Germany in the 1500s and were once used as retrievers and hunting dogs. But today the poodle is considered an ideal family dog; to many people this breed seems to have been created just to be a companion for human beings. Poodles like children, are always willing to play, and continually want to learn something new. They are usually considered the most intelligent of all dogs. Because of the present popularity of the poodle, breeders are making every effort to produce the most fashionable colors, including white, blue, brown, black, and apricot. The cut of a poodle's coat is also governed by fashion, and there are several popular styles. The photograph shows a poodle with a German cut. Poodles come in several sizes—the toy, with a shoulder height of 10 inches or under; the miniature, between 10 and 15 inches; and the standard, between 15 and 22 inches. Besides good food, regular exercise, and careful grooming, poodles need a great deal of contact with human beings.

Saluki

A saluki has the same shoulder height as a
German shepherd, but it weighs only a quarter
of what a shepherd weighs. The saluki is a
gentle, quiet dog which is good with children.
It is not attached to the house, but it forms a
very strong attachment to its master. This trait
is inherited from the saluki's ancestors, which
were the companion dogs of nomads. Salukis
originated in Syria and are the oldest purebred
dogs in the world. They were brought to Egypt
by Arab traders about 6,000 years before the
birth of Christ. They can easily be kept in
an apartment if given enough exercise. Like
greyhounds, salukis must reach a trot before
they are really exercised. A saluki's owner
should ride a bicycle for half an hour to an
hour a day, allowing the saluki to run alongside. This is good for the dog's (as well as the
master's) figure and general health. When
racing, a saluki can reach speeds of more than
30 miles an hour. Salukis do not have a typical
dog's character; they are quite independent
and usually follow orders only when they want
to. Attempting to break their will by beating
them will have disastrous results, as salukis will
turn against their torturers and bite them.

Collie

The collie, a sheepdog from Scotland, has become popular partly because of Lassie, the dog featured on television for many years. In fact, Lassie has almost become the name of the breed. Collies have not been popular pets for a very long time, although they were bred as sheepdogs about 400 years ago. The original Scottish sheepdog was crossed with a gordon setter, and from this dog collies received their coloring. From a third ancestor, the borzoi, they got their attractive build. The borzoi is a close relative of the greyhound, and this is the reason collies are shaped almost like greyhounds. However, collies are not used for running, as many greyhounds are. Collies are exceptionally affectionate dogs; they love children and do not like fighting, even in play. Although the long-haired collie is the best known, there are varieties of collies with smooth, short-haired coats. Collies with long hair need to be groomed regularly, as all long-haired dogs do. Collies should be kept in a large yard and given a comfortable mattress to sleep on. They reach a shoulder height of between 22 and 24 inches and weigh between 50 and 75 pounds.

German Shepherd

German shepherds are faithful dogs which need strong and energetic masters. Bred about 50 years ago as watchdogs and guard dogs, German shepherds have all the characteristics necessary for these jobs. They are alert, quick, and intelligent, and they can be taught to attack ferociously. In addition, their loyalty to their master knows no bounds. An attack-trained dog should never be kept as a pet; it is too powerful and is capable of causing too much harm. Such a dog should always be under strict control. If a German shepherd is to be a guard dog, it is placed in the hands of a trainer at the age of one and a half. Trained German shepherds are most often used in police work. However, dogs of this breed can also be trained as guide dogs for the blind; their intelligence and faithfulness make them especially suited for this work. If German shepherds are brought up in a loving home and not attack trained, they make friendly, loyal pets. Like all dogs they must be shown who is the master, and then they will be obedient all their lives. German shepherds need exercise; they should have an hour's walk every day.

Schnauzer

Schnauzers are always gay, lively, and fairly noisy. This breed comes in three sizes—the miniature, with a shoulder height of up to 14 inches, the standard, with a height of 14 to 19 inches, and the giant, with a height of 19 to 28 inches. All varieties share a fondness for barking and fighting. A real schnauzer will start a fight with every other dog it sees, no matter how large the dog is. And the schnauzer is often the winner in these fights. Many schnauzers, if not carefully raised, tend to roam wild. However, all these faults are easily out-weighed by the schnauzers' many good points: They love children, are always cheerful, and are easy to care for, making few demands with regard to diet, grooming, or sleeping quarters. Anyone who buys a schnauzer and raises it with strictness as well as affection will have a bright and alert companion for 12 to 14 years. This person must be prepared, however, to listen to some loud barking, especially when the schnauzer wants to go for one of his long, healthy walks. Giant schnauzers are often black, and standards are usually a salt-and-pepper color, whereas toys come in both colorings.

Saint Bernard

The Saint Bernards became famous as the search dogs of the monastery of St. Bernard, high in the Swiss Alps. They have a superior sense of smell, which makes them excellent tracking dogs. Years ago, when there were foot travelers in the Alps, men and women often lost their way or became buried under avalanches and sudden snowstorms. The monks of St. Bernard trained their dogs to rescue these unfortunate travelers. A Saint Bernard will follow a scent tirelessly and can find people even when they are buried under several feet of snow. Then it will bark loudly to call for help. Saint Bernards make excellent pets, but they need enough room to exercise. They are completely out of place in a small house or apartment. With a shoulder height of about two and a half feet and a weight of 140 to 220 pounds, this breed is one of the largest in existence. The Saint Bernard is kept throughout the world as a reliable watchdog. (Just seeing one can be threatening to some people.) A Saint Bernard puppy should be strictly trained so that it will always be obedient. Otherwise the dog's size would make it too dangerous, especially if someone it disliked came too close.

Great Dane

The Great Dane is another dog which should not be purchased as a decorative pet. These dogs reach a shoulder height of 29 to 32 inches and weigh 120 to 150 pounds. When they stand on their hind legs, they are taller than a human being. If they are strictly trained, they will obey their master's every word. A badly trained Great Dane can, however, be dangerous. If it jumps up on someone, the person will be knocked over just from the impact. If it decides to go off the path when taking a walk, the person holding the leash will simply be dragged along behind. And if it bites someone, there may be even more unpleasant consequences. We must remember that a Great Dane's head alone is longer than a toy dachshund! Its stomach is similarly proportioned; these dogs should have up to five pounds of meat a day if they are to be properly fed. The master of a Great Dane should be a tall, confident person who is a good leader and commander. If this is the case, the owner will have an excellent watchdog and an even-tempered companion who is always faithful to the family.

Pekingese

At one time Pekingese were the royal dogs of China and could be owned only by people of royal blood. They were raised inside China for hundreds of years before the rest of the world even knew of their existence. Pekingese are charming dogs which can live in even the smallest apartment or house. They do not need strenuous exercise and do not eat much. Young Pekingese must be given special care and attention because they are quite delicate. Even the grown dogs need some care; they should be groomed daily to keep their long coats attractive. Pekingese are brave, attentive watchdogs and announce any visitor loudly. Fortunately their voices are not quite so penetrating as those of other dogs which like to bark. When they are older, Pekingese often become a little sulky and unfriendly, especially to strangers and young children. However, they are always friendly to the members of the family, including the children, if they were not teased when they were young. A Pekingese needs to be active and loves to play. Such characteristics make it necessary to train these dogs well, so that they do not become too mischievous.

Pomeranian

This small, fluffy bundle of fur has a surprisingly fierce temperament. Pomeranians growl and bark menacingly at strangers, and they let themselves be petted and picked up only by their owners. The Pom gets its personality from its ancestors; it is a member of the lupine family of dogs, whose members are closer relatives of the wolf than any other dogs are. Other breeds in this family include the spitz (drawn at left), Siberian husky, Samoyed, Alaskan malamute, and chow. Since a Pom enjoys barking and is wary of strangers, it makes a good watchdog. These traits even compensate for the Pomeranian's size—it is a toy dog and reaches a shoulder height of only 11 inches. Poms do not get their full coats until they are three years old. At that time they have a manelike frill around the neck, long-haired back legs, and the bushy tail typical of the lupine family. A Pomeranian is very faithful to its owner, but young children should not come too near, as the Pom is likely to snap at them, especially if its fur is pulled. Great care must be taken that the Pom does not become too fat; this breed of dog is not very fond of exercise.

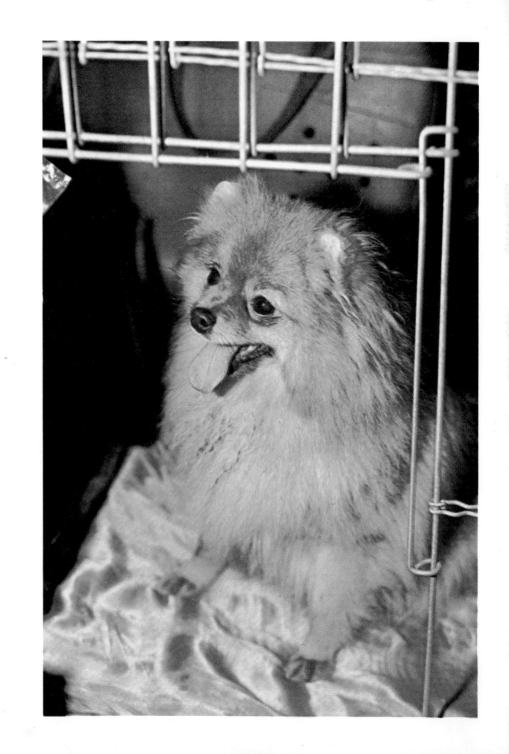

Rhesus Monkey

Like the long-tailed and the woolly monkeys, the rhesus monkey needs a very strong, large cage. It can, however, also be kept on a chain. A monkey should never have a band around its neck; it needs a harness for its chest or a broad leather belt around its stomach. The rhesus monkey should also have a tree trunk on which it can climb about. Its water and food should be put in firm, heavy containers which are fastened to the edge of the play area. Vitamins should be added daily to the water. A pet monkey's diet is made up of a rich variety of nuts, peanuts, fruit, oats, eggs, heart, and vegetables. Every kind of monkey will bite sooner or later. For this reason the person who keeps a monkey should take the precaution of having tetanus shots. Strangers should never be allowed to stroke a tame monkey—or any other tamed wild animal, for that matter. A monkey should never be kept where passersby could annoy him. Children especially are likely to tease monkeys. When a monkey is teased, its

anger builds up steadily, and finally the animal may take its rage out on some innocent person. Seldom will a monkey be completely house-trained, so it cannot be allowed to run around in the room. It is best to put gravel, sawdust, wood shavings, leaf mold, or sand in its cage, and the floor covering should be changed daily. A smooth cement floor that can be be hosed down every day is also suitable. Such intelligent animals as monkeys cannot be kept as mere decorative pets. They must be played with every day and given plenty of amusing toys so that when they are alone they have the opportunity to work off their need to play. Only a young monkey will accept a new family completely and look on his keeper as the chief of the group. Thus it is important to buy a young or at the most a half-grown animal. Monkeys can be trained to a certain extent, and they remain attached and tame if their keeper always maintains his authority and does not give in to their every whim.

Monkey

Anyone who wants to keep a monkey as a pet must realize that he is buying an animal which will have the intelligence of a three-year-old child, and he must treat the monkey accordingly. The monkey should have toys in its cage to satisfy its need for movement and to challenge its intelligence. In addition, its owner must spend a great deal of time with the animal, playing with it and training it. Monkeys often become attached to one person and then react jealously towards others and bite them. The keeper must do everything he can to force the monkey to give up its habit of biting. Even a playful young animal should not be allowed to nip at a hand or an arm. When the monkey tries to bite, rebuke it sharply and press the sides of its mouth firmly until it cries and lets go. This process is necessary only once or twice for an intelligent animal. As herd animals, monkeys are used to submitting to a social order, but they will always try to become the leader of the group. In the wild, they have fights to determine their social position within the group, and these fights are accompanied by much crying and biting. A defeated monkey shows that he wishes to give up by assuming a cowering position, and then the fight stops immediately. When a monkey is disobedient, it is probably attempting to become the boss over its keeper. Therefore any disobedience on the part of the monkey must be punished quickly and consistently. If the animal does gain the position of boss, it will not play anymore but will spend its time trying to force its will on its owner. An attacking monkey is so quick, and its teeth are so sharp, that people are soon overcome. And since human beings cannot duplicate the cowering behavior that would stop the aggression, the monkey will go on biting until its victim is seriously hurt. The best method of keeping a monkey, or any wild animal, is to spend a lot of time with it, to use strict discipline, and to give it a comfortable place to live.

Squirrel Monkey

The squirrel monkey is sometimes called the "death's head monkey" because of its pale, thin face. It comes from the jungles of South America. Like other monkeys, the squirrel monkeys are by nature herd animals and thus become very attached to their owner if they are kept alone. However, it is better for them to be kept in pairs in a large cage. If we spend a lot of time with the two monkeys, they will become just as tame as if they were by themselves. And if we do not have time for them or if we lose interest in them (which is quite possible because they usually live for many years), they will still have someone to play with. Squirrel monkeys should be given several toys that will help them occupy their time, and they should also be taught a number of tricks. These things may partially make up for the monkeys' life in captivity, which is fairly dreary in comparison to their existence in the wild. Squirrel monkeys may have the unpleasant habit of biting, and they should be forced to give this up. It is best to buy squirrel monkeys when they are young and bring them up with a varied diet of fruit, oats, meat, and insects. Vitamins must also be included in their food.

Bush Baby

This charming half-monkey from Africa cannot be kept loose in the house. All its good qualities are spoiled by its smell. The bush baby urinates over its fingers and uses them to mark off the boundaries of its living area. Thus the best thing is to give it a large cage with a tree trunk inside. The bush baby rolls itself up in its sleeping box like a marmot during the day but in the evening it becomes lively and jumps from branch to branch. Leaf mold is best for the floor as it absorbs at least a little of the smell. A bush baby is an intelligent, attentive animal which is very curious about all that goes on around it. Thus the cage should be positioned so that the bush baby can see the part of the room in which most of the activity takes place. Also, it is important to spend some time with this animal when it is awake in the evening. A bush baby's diet should be varied. It loves mealworms and can be given only them if there is nothing else at hand. But eggs, oats, sweet fruit, grasshoppers, worms, and chicken and beef heart are acceptable foods as well. Great care must be taken that these animals do not either get too fat or lose too much weight. Sometimes it is not easy to control the amount of food they get, as older animals may bite if they are displeased. However, if the bush baby is purchased when young, it gets used to being handled. In fact, many bush babies sleep during the day in their owner's pocket. It is best to buy two of these animals. They can entertain each other when no one else is around. They groom each other and play together, and they look after each other's health in a way that a human being could never do. Like all mammals, bush babies shed their coats and are especially sensitive to the wrong food at this time. Bush babies were given their name in their native country because they cry like babies at night. Fortunately this happens only during the mating season.

These plump little animals, which originally came from South America, are today bred all over the world in many varieties. The "beatle" guinea pig in the photograph has the longest hair of any breed. Guinea pigs are actually not pigs but rodents, related to mice and rats. They are often used in medical and biological experiments, and thus a "guinea pig" is anyone who is given tests or experimented upon. Because it is easy to care for, the guinea pig is an ideal first pet. By having this animal in our home, we learn the responsibilities and gentleness necessary in caring for any animal. A guinea pig's needs are quite simple. It is not very choosy about its food or its nest. Grass, clover, dandelions, carrots, fruit, and hay should be in its bowl regularly, and this diet should be supplemented with oats, corn, and sunflower seeds. In the summer a guinea pig only needs a pen which is open at the top and the bottom. The pen can simply be set on the lawn and then moved whenever the guinea pig has eaten all the grass within the enclosure. However, the guinea pig should be given some shade during the day. In the house it should have a box with sawdust or wood shavings in the bottom. The floor covering should be changed regularly so that the pen does not begin to smell. Guinea pigs breed rapidly and can have between 2 and 12 young every three or four months. Unlike many newborn animals, a guinea pig already has its coat and is able to see at birth. Guinea pigs live only for about three years, but because of their ability to reproduce rapidly, there is always a new favorite to replace the old one. Breeding guinea pigs teaches young people about basic biological processes. Also, if the animals have different colorings, we learn something about the laws of heredity. When a physical trait, like color, has two contrasting forms, one is likely to conceal the other in the offspring of animals. Black, for example, cancels out white in many members of the animal kingdom. Traits which easily reproduce themselves are said to be dominant; traits which become hidden are called recessive. Guinea pigs have been bred in many color combinations, such as the very attractive one the beatle guinea pig has in the photograph.

Albino mice are not often found in pet shops anymore; they have been pushed out by more exotic animals. And there is probably good reason for this. They tend to be smelly animals, and if they escape they behave just as badly as ordinary mice: They make their nests in a kitchen drawer or in the pantry, gnawing at everything stored there. In spite of these drawbacks, white mice make good pets for children over eight years old. It is best to buy these mice from medical or research institutes, where they are quite commonly used as test animals and are bred in large numbers. Black, blue, yellow, or spotted mice are also available. If we buy a white mouse, or better yet a pair of them, we should give them a suitable cage right away. Jam jars or old aquariums are not acceptable because they cannot be aired properly; wood or cardboard cages are not good either because they will soon be gnawed through. White mice must be kept in a wire cage, and it should

have a feeding trough and a water container that keeps the water from being dirtied. This cage should be placed in a large box containing shavings or leaf mold that can be changed quickly and easily. This is one way of keeping the inevitable mouse smell at a minimum. White mice can be fed with a special mouse food that contains all the important nutrients. For a change, give the mice carrots and fruit, nuts in the shell, and dry crusts. These things allow the mice to sharpen their teeth by gnawing. The mice should also be given a hiding place in their cage. This can be a small wooden box with a hole in it or several rags and pieces of paper that the mice can chew up and make into a nest. Mice breed rapidly, and they can have as many as 400 children, grandchildren, and great-grandchildren in one year. If they are underfed, these animals may become cannibals, eating their own young. If there are too many of them in the cage, they become nervous and do not breed correctly.

Golden Hamster

This charming little pet came originally from Syria, where in 1930 a family of golden hamsters was found living in an underground hole. From this family came the millions of golden hamsters all over the world. Hamsters are rodents which are most active at night. They will make a nest in their cage inside a small wooden box or underneath some straw, and then they will sleep through most of the day. But hamsters are so fond of exercise when they are awake that a cage is really too small for them. It is important that their cage have a wheel for the hamsters to use for running; they will cover several miles a night in this wheel. Hamsters can be kept in good health with a diet of grain, carrots, lettuce, and fruit. Like their close relatives the common hamsters, golden hamsters have the habit of filling their cheek pouches with food and carrying it off to their nests. They do this from instinct, even when fed exceptionally well. Thus it is important to check their sleeping boxes regularly and remove the food so that it does not rot.

Squirrel

Red and gray squirrels live wild in parks and woods in most areas of the world. It sometimes happens that the wind in spring blows a squirrel nest down from the trees, and in this way baby squirrels come into human hands. These helpless creatures have to be fed artificially. It is better not to give them cow's milk, but to mix pabulum or some other baby food with water and feed the squirrel with an eye dropper. A baby squirrel should be fed at least five times a day. Then its stomach should be stroked gently, to help the digestion and elimination systems to work well. Baby squirrels become very tame if we carry them around with us in a jacket pocket or apron pocket. They then become used to our smell, use us as a tree to climb on, and come back to the pocket when they are tired or sense danger. While squirrels are young they are very pleasant to have in the house, but when they grow older they develop qualities that make them undesirable houseguests. They gnaw at plants and furniture, tear the wallpaper and curtains, and mark their tree—in this instance their owner—with urine. For these reasons we should set squirrels free as soon as they can eat on their own. And they should be trained to stay out of doors. An older squirrel should never be allowed to run around freely indoors; later it might slip into the house unseen and create a mess. If the squirrel comes to a window, it should be chased away with a newspaper. The result of this training is a free wild animal living in a natural environment but accepting us as a partner in its games. Anyone who does not trust this theory and does not want to set his pet free must build a very large cage equipped with several branches for the squirrel to play in. Otherwise, it would be a torture for such a lively animal to be caged in. A varied diet which includes nuts, pine cones, wheat, sunflower seeds, fruit, and eggs is essential, but close contact with human beings is also necessary for these sociable little creatures.

Chipmunk

In recent years chipmunks have been offered for sale in pet shops more and more frequently. They should always be purchased in pairs; they are companionable animals which need playmates if they are not to pine away. They should have as large a cage as possible, and it should be furnished with branches for them to climb on. A sleeping box with a removable lid should be placed in one corner. The floor of the cage should be covered with leaf mold or sawdust, which must be changed often to avoid the chipmunks' strong smell. These frisky, cheerful animals can be kept in good health with a diet of grain, sunflower seeds, nuts, pine cones, carrots, fruit, and wild berries. In addition, they should have eggs and vitamins. However, daily supplies of food and fresh water are only the minimum requirements for keeping these pets; their health and well-being depend on many other things as well. First of all, they need sunshine, which they love, although they must always have some shade to withdraw to. Also, they must be kept away from drafts, as they catch cold easily. When we have taken care of all this, we must also satisfy the chipmunks' curiosity and their need for something to do. Their cage should always be placed where they can see what is going on around them, and they should be given things to eat that make them work. Pine cones, nuts in the shell, food in containers that must first be opened, tidbits that are difficult to reach—all these are good for them. Above all, we must not merely throw their food into the cage. The animals should take the first bite out of our hand. This is an important step in training them. Chipmunks are seldom completely comfortable with human beings, but by sharing much love we can achieve a great deal. They will not only become tame when feeding, but they will also have a genuine and loving relationship with us.

Horse

Like dogs, horses are faithful companions for human beings, and they can have just as close a relationship with us as dogs do. Horses are not only true friends, but also useful helpers. In today's world full of automobiles and tractors, horses have lost much of their former usefulness, but their value for riding is being appreciated more and more. The purchase price is actually the smallest expense the owner has when he is going to maintain a horse. Every horse needs a sturdy, sheltered stall at least 10 feet by 12 feet, with plenty of straw or shavings in the bottom. The basic feed is a good quality hay, which should be improved regularly by adding oats. (You should never give a horse sugar as a special treat, but carrots instead.) A horse should be brushed and groomed for half an hour every day, and it needs one hour's exercise either by being ridden or by being run at the end of a rope. Very few city dwellers have that much time, and for this reason they put their horses in riding stables and come out only to go riding. However, this is not exactly inexpensive; it usually costs about 50 to 100 dollars a month for each horse being stabled.

Pony

The pony is an ideal animal for anyone who has a large yard or farm and does not care about having a well-kept lawn. If they have a shelter from the wind, long-haired Shetland ponies can be kept out of doors all year round in many climates. They will get most of their food from grazing, but they should have carrots and oats to vary their diet, as well as additional good hay in the winter months. Ponies do not need a great deal of grooming; their long coats do not have to be brushed and combed very often. But the one thing they do need is personal contact. Horses are naturally herd animals, and they maintain contact with the group through two senses, hearing and touch. They need and expect this contact from human beings also. Frequent petting and stroking and friendly talk are as much a part of caring for a pony as the giving of tidbits. (Any treats should be given on the flat palm of the hand so that the animals can take them with their soft, flexible lips.) Ponies are horses which are less than 58 inches high at the withers (the ridge between the shoulder bones). In general they are quieter and less lively than horses, which can be fairly nervous, and they are therefore most suitable as companions for children. Their mood can be seen in their very expressive faces. If their ears bend forward and their eyes look large and dark, they are curious and will approach in a friendly way. But if their ears lie back and their eyes roll so that the whites show, you can expect mischief. As is true of all horses, ponies must not be approached quietly from behind. They can be frightened by this and may kick out with their hooves. Horses and ponies can also kick with their front hooves, but they do not do this as often. If we approach and stand at the side of these animals nothing can happen, as their leg joints will not allow for a sideways kick. It is better to start talking to ponies, or any tame animals, from quite a distance away, as this shows them that we are coming with only friendly intentions. Ponies usually live longer than horses and reach an age of about 25 years.

Donkey

Although donkeys are attractive, sweet little animals which are not very demanding about food and stabling, they are not at all suitable for life in a city. The donkey's cry, a long, drawn-out "hee haw," annoys nervous and harassed city dwellers so much that they will go to any lengths to get rid of the animal. It is better to keep a donkey in the country or at least in a place that is far enough away from any neighbors that no one else can hear the donkey's cries. Female donkeys are supposed to be much more quiet than males. They are also more gentle and make ideal playmates for children. Donkeys are good for riding, as they are very strong in spite of their small size. However, do not expect them to gallop; the most they can manage is a steady trot. It is especially fun to raise young donkeys. When a female is going to have young, she needs a stall that is well sheltered from the wind. Straw should be spread over the floor to make a comfortable bed. Newborn donkeys should not be ridden until they are at least two years old. Grass, thistles, hay, carrots, and cereals are adequate foods for these animals.

Parakeet

This small parrot is always a friendly and lively companion. The original parakeet (or budgerigar), which lives wild in large numbers in Australia, is a bright green, but these birds have long since been bred in many colors. The green and blue ones are very sturdy birds, whereas the white and yellow ones are a little more delicate. A parakeet should be purchased when young, and then he will grow completely accustomed to the family. Parakeets are quite clever and will learn to speak if the same words are said to them over and over. It is best to teach them in the early evening, when their attention is not taken up with many other things. Male parakeets can be recognized by the blue white skin on the top of the beak; the same area in female birds is a brownish color. Parakeets can be kept quite well in the regular cages that are on sale for them in pet shops, but they should always have something like a ladder or a seesaw to play with. They are happier if kept in pairs, although then they will become very attached to each other and not as attached to the family. And they are less likely to learn to speak. A small

mirror placed in the cage can give a single parakeet a feeling of companionship and thus replace another bird to some extent. Ready-mixed parakeet food can be bought in pet shops, but all kinds of fruit and lettuce should be added to this. Food that makes the birds work is also recommended. Fruits, seeds, willow twigs, and unripe grains from grass and cereals are all suitable for the playful needs of our lively little friend. For breeding parakeets, it is important to have a larger cage equipped with a nesting box. If the two birds get along well with each other, they soon will mate, and the female will then lay as many as five eggs in the box. She sits on the eggs and is fed by the male during this time. After 16 to 20 days little parakeets will be heard cheeping. They have no feathers when they are born and are quite helpless. They beg for food, which the parents give them after they have partly digested it themselves in their crops (special pouches in their throats). The little ones grow quickly, and soon there is a lively crowd in the cage. As soon as the birds are used to the family, they should be allowed to fly around the room once a day.

Lovebirds

These small parrots live wild in Africa but are also popular pets throughout the world. They are so companionable that they are usually kept in pairs. The two birds groom each other affectionately with their bills, and they feed each other with food that they have already partly digested. While doing this they make quite a lot of loud noise, which may not be ideal in a small house. Lovebirds should be kept in a cage, but they may be allowed to fly freely in the room for a short time each day. The curtains should be closed, however; otherwise the birds will fly straight into the window and get a concussion—if nothing worse. They can be enticed back into their cage with a whistle and some tidbits after they have had a good flight. This method of calling them is also effective if a bird has flown away outside. If it sees its old cage and hears a familiar whistle, it becomes hungry and comes back to its own feed trough. These small parrots should be fed on grains, fruit, and lettuce. In addition, they can be given willow twigs. They will peel the bark from them and eat the soft inner wood.

Amazon Parrot and Blunt-tailed Parrot

Of all the South American parrots, the Amazon parrots are the most popular as pets. There are many varieties, but they all have vivid green plumage and a bright, chirpy manner. Both Amazon and blunt-tailed parrots require special care and cannot be kept casually as mere conversation pieces. They make very good pets for a person who is lonely or shy; they will always be faithful and friendly and will also live for a long time. Complaints are often heard about the loud cries of parrots, but if you talk with them regularly and teach them words and sentences, they will chatter away quite merrily instead of screaming. Amazon and blunt-tailed parrots should be kept either chained to a swing perch or confined in a large cage that has some branches for them to climb on and gnaw at. These birds especially like nuts, sunflower seeds, fruit, and lettuce for their food. Their diet should also include berries, semi-ripe oats and wheat, as well as several kinds of seeds. All parrots are most content in light, draft-free places.

Scarlet Macaw

The largest and most colorful parrots are the members of the macaw family. In spite of their size, they can easily be kept in a small space. A parrot stand to which they are fastened by a chain is quite sufficient. It is best to attach branches to the stand as well, so that the macaw can climb about and sharpen its beak on them. Macaws come from the vast rain forests of South America, where they call to each other from the tops of trees with deafening screams. They never quite lose the habit of making these cries, so that a macaw is really not a suitable bird for a city dweller. In the wild, macaws are flock birds, which means that when they are kept in captivity they grow very attached to their keeper. Next to this person no one else is of any importance to them. They pay attention to members of the family or to strangers only when their favorite is not there. Macaws are quite jealous and often will bite a supposed rival quite sharply. Social contact is very important for all parrots. If we talk to them frequently, the young birds will soon learn to speak, and they can learn up to 20 words or more in a lifetime. They also learn to imitate sounds, which they then repeat continuously. If you have to listen to a macaw imitating a squeaky door year after year, you will soon begin to wish you had oiled the door from the start. Parrots usually live to be very old and are not susceptible to illnesses if fed properly. They should be given lettuce and willow twigs as well as sunflower seeds, nuts, and fruit of all kinds. Willow twigs are especially good because they break up the parrot's long day, as it will first take off the leaves, then the flowers, and finally the bark. Vitamins and cod liver oil are also very important, as is special molting food when the birds are shedding their feathers. When buying a parrot you should make sure that the plumage is in good condition. Feathers that are standing on end and that look ruffled are a sign of illness, and missing feathers indicate a plucker—a bird which plucks out its own feathers either because of boredom or because of an incorrect diet.

Chinese Nightingale

In their native home Chinese nightingales live in low bushes and eat many kinds of insects. In captivity, they should be fed with the "soft-billed" bird food that can be purchased in pet shops. Their diet must be supplemented with apples, pears, oranges, and berries. These lively birds should not be kept singly but in pairs. Their cage should be roomy; 40 inches long, 10 inches wide, and 20 inches high would be the smallest possible dimensions. The birds should be able to fly as far as possible between their perches, which should be of various thicknesses and should spring back lightly when the birds land on them. Chinese nightingales like to take baths, so they should be provided with a large bathing area and with plenty of water. The tray on the floor of the cage can be filled with sand, and the top layer taken away every day with the wasted food and droppings. It is very difficult to tell the two sexes of the Chinese nightingale apart; the females are only a little paler in color. Because of this similarity, males often must be marked with a stamp under the wing. But both sexes will sing merrily all day long.

Mynah

The mynah bird, which comes originally from India and other parts of Asia, is an extremely talented bird as far as speaking is concerned. Even at a zoo, where there are thousands of different visitors, this bird will pick up words from the public and learn to say them. Although the mynah learns whistles or whistled songs more easily than anything else, it still is better than most parrots at learning words. There are two kinds of mynah birds; one is about the size of a pigeon, and the other the size of a crow. Both have similar characteristics: They are alert, curious, and very lively. However, they do not need too large a cage, as they enjoy hopping from branch to branch but do not like flying very much. A cage about a yard long is usually large enough for them. Mynahs are easy to feed, requiring only soft-billed bird foods, cottage cheese, and fruit such as bananas, oranges, pears, plums, and grapes. Learning these facts, you may think: What could be nicer than buying one of these black creatures and keeping it as a pet in my room? However, as soon as you do, you will find out that mynah birds are very messy. They pick up their food with their beaks and throw it around the room. Also, they make a lot of droppings, so that their cage must be cleaned out every day to prevent a strong odor from developing. You can save a lot of disappointment when choosing a bird to keep as a pet if you know beforehand how much dirt you will have to accept—and also how much noise you and your neighbors must accept. These considerations are very important in buying birds like mynahs and parrots—birds which live for a long time; the enthusiasm the owner feels at first may not last a lifetime. It would be extremely cruel (and it would also show that we are not fit to keep a pet) if we had one of these dependent, intelligent birds put away, or if we sold it on short notice, just because it got on our nerves. We can avoid making a decision we will later regret by going to see the bird in the shop on several different days and at various times of the day. We should make the decision to buy only after gathering enough information to know what to expect.

Magpie

All members of the crow family, including the magpie, the jay, the raven, and the rook, are suitable as tame pets. But they make the best pets when they are taken into captivity at the right time. They should be young enough that they have to be lifted out of the nest, but they should already have grown their feathers. Or they should be young birds which have just recently flown out of the nest. Magpies and other birds which have been out of the nest a fairly long time and are almost fully grown before they are captured seldom lose their shyness of human beings. On the other hand, birds which are taken before they have grown their feathers often suffer later from feeding troubles. When you bring your fledgling home it will be eagerly begging for food, with beak open wide. Cottage cheese, meat, and egg, mixed with oats, will satisfy the bird's appetite and provide the proper nourishment. Birds of the magpie's size should be kept as pets only if they can be made so tame that they fly around the yard and always remain near the house. Once they are grown they should never be allowed in the house. If they are, they may later enter the neighbors' homes and try to steal things from them.

Canary

There are many stories about canaries who had heart attacks because they did not get their regular food at exactly the right time. These unfortunate birds were undoubtedly so bored in their dreary caged existence that their feeding time was the only bright spot in their long day. The canary is supposed to make us happy with his gay song, and it does this best of all when not distracted by anything. However, we must offer the bird some change. After all, a canary is not a machine but a living creature which has a right to be treated as such. Canaries that are good singers are very expensive, but the price is worth it—a male canary can live for 25 years and will sing day after day. The birds do not sing in the molting seasons, which are February to March and July to August. A complete change of feathers is very tiring for the birds, and we must be careful to feed them well and correctly during these times. They should have eggs and a special molting food so that they get all the basic things they need for their new plumage. The regular daily diet for canaries consists of various mixed seeds to which we should add grass seed, lettuce leaves, chickweed, dandelion leaves, and other greens. Canaries need fresh water daily in their drinking bowls and bathing containers. Often these birds are shy at first, and it is said that they are not very intelligent. An attentive and loving keeper will, however, soon win their confidence. He should never approach the cage and start to do something there unannounced; he should always talk softly to the birds beforehand so that they are not frightened. If tidbits are given on the hand, canaries will soon become tame enough for hand feeding. This is important because it is necessary to take the birds in the hand to cut their toenails and beaks. These things are not worn down sufficiently in a small cage and grow so quickly that they must be trimmed regularly. This process will be easy when the canaries have enough confidence in their keeper.

European Goldfinch

The European goldfinch lives in Europe, Asia, and northwestern Africa. It was introduced into the United States in the early 1800s and became established on Long Island. This colorful bird appears in the autumn in large flocks but lives in pairs during the rest of the year. Both the European goldfinch and the American goldfinch, which is yellow and black in color, eat seeds from thistle heads. It is difficult to tell the two sexes of the European goldfinch apart. Usually the males are more colorful, but on the other hand, old females are more colorful than young males. Since both sexes sing and chirp merrily in the cage, it does not really matter which you buy. It is best to purchase these birds in pairs. Experienced breeders let their birds fly freely in the autumn. First one of the pair is allowed to fly, and when it has returned to its partner the other is let loose. The European goldfinches are supposed to be so faithful to their mates that they will always return voluntarily to the cage. During these free flights the goldfinches catch some of their natural food, including aphids and tiny spiders. This helps them last the winter with their relatively monotonous diet of seed. And they may even breed in the spring.

Siskin

All the qualities anyone could want in a pet bird are united in the siskin. It costs very little, is always healthy, lives for a long time, and makes no great demands as far as food and living quarters are concerned. Most important of all, the siskin is always cheerful and happy. It plays around in its cage and chirps and sings all day long. By nature a flock bird, the siskin easily forms an attachment with its keeper, even if it is fairly old when it joins the family. Siskins are native to Europe, where they skim along woodland streams in summer and winter, looking for their favorite food, the fruit of the alder tree. In captivity siskins eat grains, seeds, and food for soft-billed birds. When buying a siskin, look for a young male bird which, just like the female, is a gray green color with stripes on its sides and chest. Males can always be recognized by their deeper, more yellowy color and by the dark feathers on their head. You can, of course, also choose a particularly beautiful yellow green older male bird with a jet black hood, but remember that he will not live as long as a young bird.

Butterfly Finch

The butterfly finch is a guest in our cages which is imported from East Africa. There are two subspecies of this finch, one in which the male has a red spot on his cheek and one in which he has not. The females in both varieties look very much alike and are of a duller blue color and have more gray feathers than the males. In their native habitat, butterfly finches are found in large flocks, and they should never be kept alone in captivity. If we do not want to keep more than one pair, we should mix them with some other kinds of finches. Butterfly finches are small, delicate birds which, like most of the exotic varieties, need special care. Their food must be varied, from several kinds of grain to crushed hemp and sunflower seeds. In the summer they can have unripe seeds from grass and plantain. Lettuce leaves, dandelion leaves, chickweed, soft-billed bird foods, eggs, and occasionally a leaf with aphids should also be part of their diet. During their two molting seasons each year they should have special molting food. Butterfly finches enjoy bathing, and they need a place to bathe other than their water container.

Mandarin Duck

Anyone who wants to keep water birds must have a large yard, for even small ducks, like the mandarin duck from East Asia or its relative the wood duck from North America, need two to three square yards of water for each bird. This is because ducks make a great deal of dirt, and the more water there is, the better the natural biological cleansing processes work. (Healthy bodies of water contain bacteria that break down wastes and clean up the water.) But if you have a pond in which the water is constantly being recirculated, it can be smaller. A sand filter can be built alongside to remove the impurities before the water is pumped back into the pond. The mandarin duck, like the wood duck, often makes a nest in a hollow tree. When the eggs hatch, the young ducklings jump out of the tree and waddle to the water. All ducks learn to swim much sooner than they learn to fly. To get ducks used to captivity it is best to build a wire mesh flying area around the pond and clip their wings. The wire is taken down later, when the ducks have become used to their keepers. They will eventually be so faithful to their home ground that they will come flying back every time.

Emerald Lizard

While out walking you may find lizards that you would like to observe more closely. The best way to do this is in a terrarium. Be careful when catching lizards not to pick them up by the tail, as it may break off. This is a protection for the lizard, as the tail continues wiggling and fools the enemy (you) into thinking that it is the actual lizard. The lizard later grows another tail, but it is a little smaller. In the wild, lizards like to lie flat on stones in the hot sunshine. At home in a terrarium, however, they should never be placed in the strong sun, because the heat can easily build up inside the container and kill the lizards. The terrarium should imitate the natural surroundings of the lizard; it should contain large stones with patches of dry grass or desert plants between them. Lizards need a bowl of fresh water, and they eat mealworms, grasshoppers, flies, and spiders. It is best to let lizards free in September and catch new ones in the spring. But these animals can be kept over the winter in an unheated but frost-free room.

Tree Frog

This little frog is supposed to be able to forecast the weather by changing color. The tree frog usually does turn bright green on sunny days and gray on cloudy days. But its weather predictions are no more reliable than those on the radio. On the other hand, a tree frog's color is a good indication of its mood. If it is feeling satisfied and happy, it turns bright, shining colors. If the frog is angry or upset, it becomes a dull gray black. Tree frogs also have the surprising ability to change color to match their backgrounds, which gives them good camouflage. Another unusual characteristic of this frog is the male's loud mating call in spring. When he croaks he blows up his yellow throat pouch, and it acts like an echo chamber for the sound. Tree frogs, like most pet frogs, can be fed on flies and small grasshoppers. Keeping these animals through the winter is fairly difficult. They should be put in a container with moss or leaves and kept in a frost-free room. The winter quarters must never dry out, but they also must not be kept too wet. It may be best to set the frog free after the summer is over and then buy a new one in the spring.

Turtle

These small green turtles are quite popular and can be purchased in any pet shop. Every year thousands of them are sold to would-be pet owners, but they are very difficult to keep successfully. They can easily be fed with worms and tubifex (small worms used as food for aquarium fish), but they need heated water, or they will catch cold and die. Since they quickly dirty the water, there should be nothing in their aquarium except stones, floating plants, and a floating island on which the turtles can rest in the sun. The container should be emptied every few days, scrubbed carefully, and filled again with warm water. Turtles remain healthy only if they have fresh water all the time. Otherwise their eyes swell and inflame and finally stick together. Then the unfortunate animals die. The turtles' diet should include chopped heart, tubifex, worms, snails, fruit, and lettuce leaves. Their food should always be varied. These animals, which come from the southern United States and Mexico, are lively in winter and in summer. As often as possible the container with the turtles should be placed in the sun. The harsh midday sun should be avoided, however; it may make the water too hot. Well-fed turtles grow quickly and reach a shell diameter of up to eight inches. Then they need a larger container. If you have limited space, it may be best to try to find out the name of a turtle keeper who is interested in larger turtles. This can probably be done through a pet shop. If you have a more unusual kind of turtle, you may be able to give it to a zoo. Attempts at breeding turtles can be very interesting. You will then need a larger container in order to give the turtles enough room for their lively courting games. They also should have a beach to land on that is covered with soft soil and moss. This will provide the female turtle with a place to bury the eggs. The eggs must not be touched, and certainly not taken from their places, or they will die.

Tortoise

The tortoise is a good companion even for small children, and it is easy to care for. It eats lettuce leaves, fruit, and fresh dandelions, and it should also be given small snails, meat, and hard-boiled eggs. If your floor is not too cold you do not even need a box for this animal. However, if you are going to keep the pet for a long time it is better to give it a box filled with sand. Underneath the sand, install a heating cable to keep the floor of the box warm. As often as possible the tortoise should be let out in the sun on the lawn. There it can look for the kinds of grass it prefers. Also, a tortoise needs sun for its well-being; young ones especially are very prone to rickets, a disease caused by a deficiency of vitamin D. To help combat this, they should also have vitamins in their feed regularly. Tortoises can be kept awake through the winter, but in the wild they hibernate, and a winter's sleep is good for them. To prepare a tortoise for hibernation, keep it from eating anything for a few days in November, give it a warm bath in a shallow bowl, and then put it in a box full of dry leaves in the cellar or in a closet.

Goldfish

Most of the people who are interested in aquarium fish begin their careers with a goldfish. This undemanding creature will survive even in a totally dirty and slimy bowl with the cheapest of food. However, we can have real pleasure from the goldfish only if we look after it with the same care we would give any other fish. The bowl must not be too small, as goldfish grow up quickly to about four to six inches in length. A good filter with active charcoal takes away most of the solid and some of the dissolved waste and keeps the water clear in spite of the activity of the fish. Good ventilation with an air pump is important, especially if many fish are in the aquarium. If the fish are swimming up to the surface of the aquarium too often, this is a sign that they are not getting enough oxygen and that better ventilation is needed. Hardy and quick-growing plants make the aquarium attractive and provide some oxygen in the water for the fish. It is best to let the plants start to grow before the fish are put into the aquarium, as goldfish like to look for food on the bottom, and they often uproot plants that are not securely attached. Vallisneria and elodea are two plants especially good for the goldfish bowl, and they grow quickly again when the fish have eaten at them. Well-ventilated and filtered water is biologically so active that it cleans itself and does not have to be changed frequently. If the waste material is filtered out regularly, it is sufficient if a third of the water is replaced each month. Continually disturbing the water is not only troublesome to the keeper but is also not good for the plants and the fish. Goldfish originally came from China and were bred from a colorless member of the carp family. Over the years the Chinese have created a series of odd-shaped fish from this ordinary one—monsters with bulbous eyes, huge bellies, bumps on their heads, and egglike shapes. Many of them can hardly even swim. The most beautiful results of hundreds of years of careful breeding are the charming veiltails, fish with large flowing fins and tails. All the special breeds need a higher water temperature and cleaner water than ordinary goldfish do.

Guppy

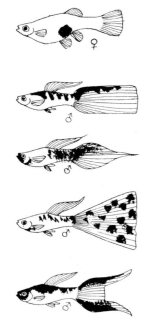

Guppies, whose native home is in the warm fresh waters of Central and South America, are the most popular aquarium fish. They are very easy to care for and can even be kept on dry food in an unheated aquarium. They are also quite easy to breed. Their great productivity makes them especially interesting to anyone who wants to create new varieties. A systematic application of the laws of heredity is certain to bring exciting results. A female guppy can have between 50 and 100 young every three or four weeks, and in a short time these young will also reproduce actively. For this reason the guppy is sometimes called the "millions fish." Guppies are unusual fish because they are viviparous; they produce live young directly from their bodies. (Most kinds of fish lay eggs.) The female guppies are larger than the males and are grayish green with no distinctive markings. The males, on the other hand, grow to only three-fourths of an inch long and come spotted and streaked in the most improbable colors. In addition, a wide variety of fin shapes has been developed in the males. Although guppies can survive with little care, they should be given plant food and live food, as well as good quality dry food, to keep them in good health.

Paradise Fish

This fish is called the paradise fish because the male develops a marvelous variety of colors during the mating season and while the young fish are hatching. One other factor makes this fish a desirable addition to an aquarium; it is not too particular about the temperature and cleanliness of the water. Paradise fish come from the rice fields of Southeast Asia and their breathing system is adapted to bad water conditions. In addition to their gills they have a lung system that enables them to take in oxygen directly from the air. They are so dependent on their extra breathing equipment that they will die if the way to the surface of the water is blocked. Even though a small, unheated aquarium is enough for them to live in, only when the water is heated do they develop their most interesting characteristics. Paradise fish are happiest in a fairly warm aquarium that contains many floating plants and has room in the middle for their games. Male paradise fish engage in fights to determine their relative social positions and are quite fierce towards each other. But if the aquarium is large enough, no one will be hurt. When two rivals meet, they spread their fins and swim towards each other with their gills thrust forward. They swim side by side through the water, and each tries to convince the other of his strength by taking strong strokes with his fins. If this is not successful, a fight is necessary to settle the question. The rivals bite each other and push and pull each other through the water. As soon as one fish's superior strength has been determined, the weaker fish pulls in his fins. This act of submission causes the other fish to stop fighting also. The paradise fish are even more interesting when they are courting. The male spreads his fins out until they almost tear as he circles around his chosen lady. Finally he embraces her under a nest of air bubbles that he prepared earlier and she lays the eggs. This is the end of her part, for it is the male's duty to guard the nest and the eggs. While the eggs are maturing, he replaces any air bubbles that break. After the fish hatch, he cares for the young for three or four days. But then his fatherly instincts leave him and he must be taken away, as he often develops cannibalistic tendencies.

Angelfish

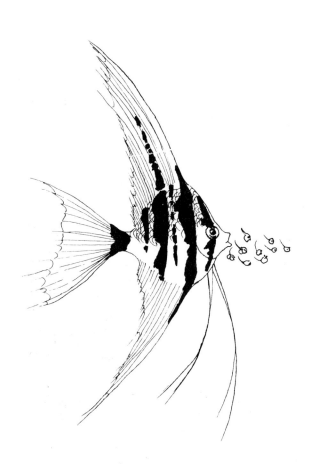

The beautiful angelfish can easily be kept in an aquarium with any other fish, except for the neon tetra. The brilliant red and blue tetra seem to be part of the angelfish's food in its home territory, the Amazon River region. Angelfish thrive only if they have live food in a well-planted larger aquarium, and they also need to have the water temperature between 75 and 82 degrees. At breeding time, the males and females choose partners and separate from the other fish. They clean a stone or a hard leaf and lay the eggs there. When the new fish hatch, the parents take them one by one into their mouths and carefully remove all remaining egg. Then they spit the young fish into a sand pit. The young are not allowed to leave this area until they are completely able to swim. Even when they are older they stay in a group near their parents and return to the pit at night. Angelfish have a well-developed system of communication: They do not use language, but they "talk" by swimming, by making special movements, and by changing color. For this reason they offer the observer opportunities to try to understand the emotional and social existence of a kind of life that is very foreign to ours.

On the following pages I have compiled a general list of the most important tips for the upkeep of these animals. The list includes many of the points that have already been mentioned in the individual descriptions. The purchase prices are given as a range from the least expensive to the most expensive. As far as food is concerned, I have mentioned only the items that are absolutely necessary for the well-being of the animals. Any other foods that the animals like and that brighten up their day are sincerely recommended. Lettuce, which is a common pet food, can easily be enriched by the addition of dandelions and other greens. Even unconventional foods like table scraps can be given to the animals if they like them and do not get too much of them. The tortoise in the photograph on page 97 has lived for more than 35 years with some friends of mine, and any animal diet specialist would probably be surprised to see the things that animal eats. The amount of space a pet needs also varies greatly. The less time we have to spend with them, the more room they need to play in. Above all, it is important always to remember that good pet keeping does not depend on the physical things, such as food, water, and bedding, but on the intangibles, such as love and tenderness. This love cannot be an egotistic love, in which we see the animals just as objects or possessions, but it must be a true deep-seated affection that gives the animal the best basis for a long and happy life. For only when we try to understand the animal and appreciate its own life style will the pleasure and the affection be truly mutual. It is difficult to generalize about how long pets will live. Some pets which are loved especially well and are looked after carefully reach an age that is well above the average, but others which are less fortunate die much sooner.

Animal	Requirements	Food	Approximate Cost	Where to Buy
house cat	room, yard	milk, meat, canned food	$0-10	cat lovers, animal home
Siamese cat	room, yard	milk, meat, canned food	$25-35	pet shop, breeder
Persian cat	room	milk, meat, canned food	$0-25	pet shop, breeder, cat lovers
small dog	room, yard if watched	meat, bones, commercially prepared food	$25-150	pet shop, breeder
large dog	yard	meat, bones, commercially prepared food	$50-250	pet shop, breeder
monkey	cage, room if watched	eggs, oats, fruit, nuts, insects	$30-200	pet shop

Animal	Requirements	Food	Approximate Cost	Where to Buy
rodent	cage, room if watched	oats, seeds, fruit, nuts, vegetables	$2-5	pet shop
horse	stable, field	hay, oats, grass, carrots	$200-1,000	horse dealer, breeder
pony	field, sheltered corner	hay, grass, clover, carrots	$100-500	horse dealer, breeder
donkey	grassy area, sheltered corner	hay, grass, carrots	$100-400	horse dealer, breeder
small parrots	cage, room	seeds, nuts, fruit, lettuce	$25-70	pet shop
large parrots	cage, room	seeds, nuts, fruit, lettuce	$90-300	pet shop
seed-eating birds	cage	seeds, fruit, lettuce	$5-15	pet shop

Animal	Requirements	Food	Approximate Cost	Where to Buy
soft-billed birds	cage	insects, soft foods, eggs, cottage cheese, fruit, lettuce	$5-10	pet shop
mynah	cage, room to fly	meat, insects, eggs, fruit, cottage cheese, oats, lettuce	$50-100	pet shop
lizard	terrarium	insects, mealworms, snails	$1-5	pet shop
frog	terrarium	flies, mealworms	$1-4	pet shop
tortoise	terrarium or box	eggs, lettuce, fruit, snails	$10-15	pet shop
turtle	terrarium with water	fish, meat, worms	$1-2	pet shop
fish	aquarium	water fleas, dried and living food	$.25-5.00	pet shop

NATURE AND MAN

Books in This Series

AMONG THE PLAINS INDIANS, a fictional account based on the actual travels of two explorers who observed American Indian life in the 1830's, features illustrations by artists George Catlin and Karl Bodmer.

AQUARIUM FISH from Around the World presents an exciting picture of the varied species of fish that inhabit the miniature world of an aquarium.

BIRDS OF THE WORLD in Field and Garden combines colorful photographs and an informative text to describe some of the world's most interesting birds.

CREATURES OF POND AND POOL describes many of the beautiful and unusual creatures—frogs, water snakes, salamanders, aquatic insects—that live in and around fresh-water ponds.

DOMESTIC PETS describes the special characteristics of the animals which can live comfortably and happily with man, including several kinds of dogs, cats, birds, monkeys, reptiles, and fish.

WILD ANIMALS OF AFRICA takes the reader on a safari with German naturalist Klaus Paysan, who tells of his adventures in Africa and describes the living habits of the continent's most fascinating animals.

These fact-filled books contain more than fifty four-color plates and over 100 pages. Printed on high quality paper and reinforced bound, these books will add an exciting new dimension to any collection.

For more information about these and other quality books for young people, please write to

LERNER PUBLICATIONS COMPANY

241 First Avenue North, Minneapolis, Minnesota 55401

An African leopard, a photograph from *Wild Animals of Africa*